This Book
Belongs To

_____

Based on the "Winnie the Pooh" works by A.A. Milne and E.H. Shepard

First Edition
Library of Congress Cataloging-in-Publication Data on file.
ISBN 978-1-4231-3591-3

G942-9090-6-11032

Manufactured in the USA

For more Disney Press fun, visit www.disneybooks.com

SUSTAINABLE FORESTRY INITIATIVE
Certified Fiber Sourcing
www.sfiprogram.org
PWC-SFICOC-260

For Text Pages Only

Table of Contents

Disney
Winnie the Pooh

A Hundred-Acre Wood
Treasury

Buzzzzzzzzzzzz

ADAPTED BY Lisa Ann Marsoli

ILLUSTRATED BY Mario Cortes, Valeria Turati,
Olga Mosqueda and the Disney Storybook Artists

Disney PRESS
NEW YORK

Come along with Winnie the Pooh and share in all the simple joys found just around every corner of the Hundred-Acre Wood . . . a delightful world where curiosity takes flight and friendships abound.

In this latest addition to the tales of the bear-of-very-little-brain, the adventures that have delighted generations continue.

To many, these friends—from lovable Pooh, loyal Piglet, and glum Eeyore to clever Christopher Robin, kind Kanga, and playful Roo to bouncy Tigger, practical Rabbit, and wise old Owl—are as familiar and as cherished as members of their own family.

It's no wonder that every generation loves sharing Winnie the Pooh with the next!

Something Is Missing!

There once was a boy named Christopher Robin who had a room full of wonderful toys to play with. Of all of these, the stuffed animals were his favorites—especially a bear called Winnie the Pooh.

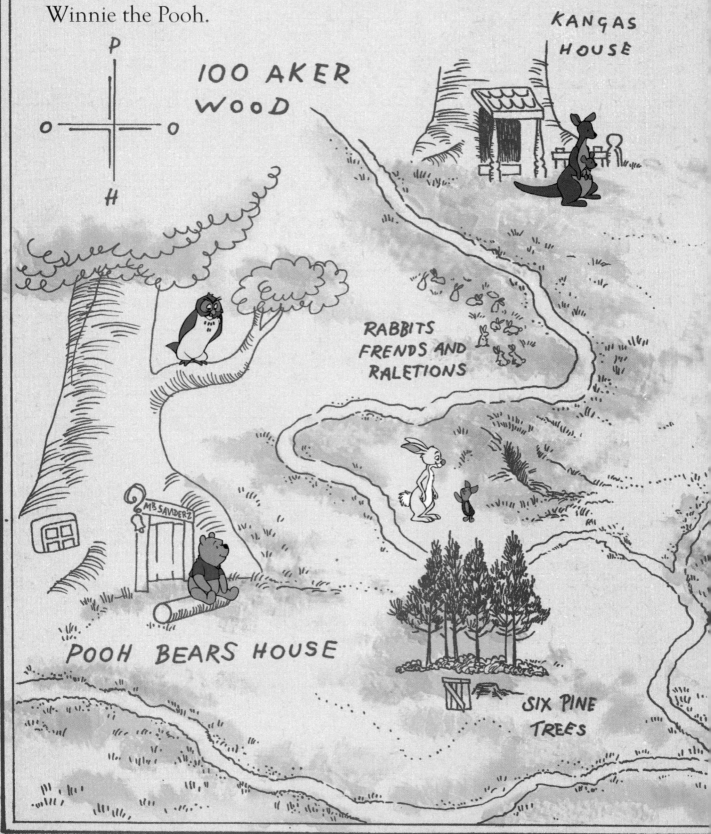

100 AKER WOOD

KANGAS HOUSE

RABBITS FRENDS AND RALETIONS

MR SAUNDERZ

POOH BEARS HOUSE

SIX PINE TREES

The boy, Pooh, and the rest of their well-worn friends

spent many happy hours sharing make-believe adventures

in a beautiful place called the Hundred-Acre Wood.

MR SHEPARD HELPD

Early one morning, Pooh slept in his cozy house inside a tree dreaming of honey. Honey was his favorite thing to think and dream about, as well as his favorite thing to eat. And on those rare occasions when Pooh forgot about honey, his rumbly tummy was quick to remind him.

On this day, Pooh woke up to discover that his tummy was complaining especially loudly. He knew that the only way to quiet it was to fill it with lots of delicious honey.

As Pooh dressed, he and his tummy sang a song together that included reassuring words like "sweet" and "eat." (Well, actually Pooh sang the words, while his tummy made musical sounds, like GURGLE! and POP!)

Finally, it was time for breakfast. Pooh checked his cupboard first, sure there would be a pot full of the sweet stuff.

"Empty," observed Pooh. "Well, luckily, I keep some extra in the house."

Pooh continued his search, checking under his bed and on the ledge above his door. Unfortunately, every honeypot he found was lacking the "honey" part.

Finally, he came upon a jar he felt sure was full.

He tipped it back farther . . . and farther . . . and farther . . .
until the weight of the pot *tipped* him right over!

Sensing that Pooh had been distracted from his task, his stomach issued forth several more hungry and impatient sounds.

Pooh realized that drastic measures were in order. Since there was no honey to be found inside, he had no choice but to venture out into the Hundred-Acre Wood to find some more.

Suddenly, Pooh spotted some bees. Since where there were bees, there was usually honey, Pooh felt hopeful—and a little cautious. He had learned from experience that beehives could be very unfriendly places when the bees were home!

Buzz

Buzz

Buzz

What he needed, Pooh decided, was a disguise. He spotted a tree branch and held it in front of him. Now the bees would think he was a tree branch, too.

Buzz

Buzz

Buzz

Pooh reached inside the beehive.

Buzzzzzzzzzzzz

But the bees were not fooled—most likely

because tree branches don't reach into beehives!

A big, angry swarm poured out of the hive, and Pooh took off running. He knew he couldn't out-run the bees, so he would have to out-think them—which was no small task for a bear-of-very-little-brain.

Buzzzzzz

Luckily he stumbled upon the perfect hiding spot.
He vowed that just as soon as the bees were gone, he
would pay his friends a visit. Surely one of them would
have some honey to spare.

In another part of the Hundred-Acre
Wood, Eeyore was greeting the day by saying,
"Why?" And then, "What's the point?"

By the time Pooh came upon Eeyore, the donkey was thoughtfully chewing on some thistles.

"Good morning, Eeyore," said Pooh. "You wouldn't happen to have any honey lying about, would you?"

Without waiting for an answer, Pooh crawled inside the
front of Eeyore's house to have a look for himself. When he
didn't find what he was looking for, Pooh's tummy suggested
that he check the back of Eeyore's house.

Pooh came out empty-handed, finally stopping to take a good, long look at his friend.

"Eeyore," said Pooh, "what has happened to your tail?"

"What *has* happened to it?" Eeyore wondered.

"Well, it isn't there," Pooh explained.

"What *is* there?" asked Eeyore.

"Nothing," replied Pooh.

"That accounts for a good deal," observed Eeyore.

Pooh knew what he had to do. "I, Winnie the Pooh,
will find your tail," he promised. "And then we shall get
some honey."

Just then, a familiar voice drifted

d
o
w
n

to them from a nearby tree.

"'Chapter One: The Birth of a Genius,'"
it began. "'A breezy wind whiffed through
the wood . . .'"

"Pardon me, Owl," interrupted Pooh.

"What are you doing?"

"Hmmm? Oh, hello, Pooh, Eeyore," Owl said.
"Why, I'm penning my personal memoirs."

"Perhaps you could take a short break from
your important work and help us find Eeyore's
tail?" asked Pooh. "You have such a talent for
speaking and telling us what to do."

Owl handed Pooh a pad and pencil. "Write this down carefully," he instructed. "Now the customary procedure in such cases is as follows . . ."

"What does '*crustimony proceedcake*' mean?" Pooh asked.

Owl explained it meant "the thing to do" and continued, "The thing to do is as follows: first, issue a reward. . . ."

On hearing the word "issue," Pooh said, "Gesundheit."

"I beg your pardon?" replied Owl.

"You sneezed just as you were going to tell me what the first thing to do was," Pooh said.

"I didn't sneeze," disagreed Owl. "As I was saying, first, issue a reward. . . ."

"He's doing it again," Pooh told Eeyore. He turned to Owl. "You must be catching a cold."

"I'm not catching a cold," Owl insisted. "The word is 'issue,' not 'achoo.'"

"My throat feels a little scratchy," Eeyore admitted.

"Just as I suspected," Pooh said. "Owl, we need honey."

Owl's patience was at an end. "Enough of this infernal folderol! Look, the thing to do is, we write a notice promising a large something to anyone who finds a replacement tail for Eeyore. Is that clear?"

"Oh, that sounds like a wonderful plan, Owl," said Pooh, imagining a tasty honey reward as he listened.

"Excellent!" replied Owl. "Now, we shall get
Christopher Robin to write out the notices, and
we'll put them up all over the forest."

And with that, he flew off to the boy's
house to ask for his help.

Christopher Robin immediately set to work making several large signs that read A VERY IMPORTANT THING TO DO. Each one had a spelling mistake or two, but since no one in the Hundred-Acre Wood was any better at spelling, it was certain that no one would notice.

Pooh helpfully took the signs and began posting them all around the Hundred-Acre Wood.

As Pooh was hammering one of the notices onto a tree, he thought he heard a low, growling sound.

"Is that you, tummy?" he asked.

When Pooh's tummy didn't answer, he finished posting the signs and turned to leave, bumping directly into B'loon. Just as Pooh was inviting him along for the Very Important Thing To Do today, Tigger leaped out of a bush and pounced on B'loon.

"Whew! That was a close call there, Pooh Bear. This guy was about to pounce the stuffing outta you!"

B'loon wasted no time in slipping out from Tigger's hold. The two wrestled, but hard as he tried, Tigger could not escape B'loon's sticky, tricky hold on him.

"Don't be afraid, Tigger," said Pooh. "It's only B'loon."

Tigger assured Pooh that he was only pretending to be afraid. . . .

"So's my opponent would *underestimize* me, and then I'd get the drop on him! Well, I think this little guy's learned his lesson. There may be others out there in harm's way, so I must go . . . because the Hundred-Acre Wood needs a hero . . . and I'm the only one!"

And with that, Tigger bounced off into the Wood.

Christopher Robin waited for all his friends to arrive, then called the meeting about the Very Important Thing To Do to order. He gestured to Eeyore, who turned to display his barren backside. "We will have a contest to find a new tail for Eeyore," Christopher Robin said.

Owl interrupted to remind Christopher Robin that contests usually involved some kind of prize for the winner.

Everyone had a different idea as to what a desirable prize might be.

Pooh gave Christopher Robin the piece of paper with his drawing. The boy smiled. "Why, Pooh, that's a grand idea!" he exclaimed. "The prize for a new tail shall be a pot of honey!"

Disney

Winnie the Pooh

Tails, Tricks, and Traps

Pooh picked up a pinecone from the ground and examined it. Would this make a suitable tail for Eeyore? he wondered.

Suddenly, Pooh had a better idea. "I have just the thing!"
he exclaimed. He dashed toward home, where the most perfect
tail he could think of was hanging on his wall.

"Thanks, Pooh," said Eeyore after Pooh had outfitted him with a clock. The friends declared Pooh the contest winner.

Then they presented hungry Pooh with his reward—a nice, full pot of delicious honey!

But before Pooh could scoop out even one pawful of the
gooey stuff— CRUNCH! —Eeyore had sat on his clock tail
and crushed it.

CRUNCH!

"Oh, dear," Owl said. And with that, he snatched the
honeypot back from a very disappointed (and still very
hungry) Pooh.

"We could give B'loon a try," suggested Piglet. But as he carried his round, red friend over to Eeyore, Piglet's feet lifted off the ground.

"Whoa!" he cried with alarm.

Luckily, Christopher Robin caught him.

The boy tied the bright red balloon to Eeyore's bottom. "What do you think, Eeyore?" he asked.

Eeyore discovered the problem with having a balloon for a tail is that you have to go where it wants to go—and not the other way around!

"Whoopsie," said Christopher Robin. He pulled Eeyore back to earth and untied the balloon. "Let's try something else. Thanks, B'loon.

Good-bye!"

The friends tried a
great many more things
for Eeyore's tail:

a yo-yo,

an umbrella,

a weather vane,

a party hat,

a moose head,

and an accordion

... until at last they ran out of them. "It's okay," said Eeyore. "I'll learn to live without it."

Kanga felt terrible seeing Eeyore so downcast. "Poor dear," she said. "I may have just the thing." She attached her scarf to Eeyore's backside. "There you are."

"Why, Kanga!" Christopher Robin exclaimed. "It appears that you are the winner!"

Owl presented her with the prize.

Pooh's tummy, meanwhile, was feeling a
little eleven-o'-clockish—which meant that it
was demanding something to eat. Pooh went
off to look for honey again, but he was finding
his stomach's ruckus very distracting indeed.

Pooh noticed a piece of yarn lying on the ground. He picked it up and followed it . . . straight to Eeyore.

But Eeyore was unaware that he was dragging something along with him.

Pooh tried to warn him, but he was

knocked
right
off his
feet!

When Pooh landed, he found himself quite close to
Christopher Robin's house. "Christopher Robin will have
some honey!" he declared.

Christopher Robin was not there, but he had left a note
on the door. Pooh was puzzled. He decided to take the note
to Owl's house.

Pooh arrived just in time to see Owl being presented with the prize for finding Eeyore's latest tail.

"Let me see," said Owl. "There's never been a note written that I could not decipher." He placed the honey on the mantle and invited Pooh to help himself.

"It says," began Owl, "'Gone out, busy Backson. Signed, Christopher Robin.' Our dear friend Christopher Robin has been captured by a creature called the Backson!"

The friends gasped in fear.

"It's malicious," Owl added, "ferocious, and worst of all . . . terribly busy! I saw a picture of one just the other day."

While Owl was speaking, Pooh had been stacking books to climb on in order to reach Owl's honey. Now, Owl pulled the books out from under Pooh, looking for the one that contained a picture of the Backson. Pooh was right back where he started!

"Dash it all!" Owl complained. "Where is that picture?"

"Can you draw it?" asked Roo, offering Owl a piece of chalk.

Owl drew a frightening monster with shaggy fur, horns, and a ring in its nose—and assured his friends that the beast was also extremely smelly.

Now that everyone knew what a Backson looked like, they were curious to find out what one actually *did*.

Owl described a thoughtless creature that scribbled in library books, spoiled milk, stopped clocks,

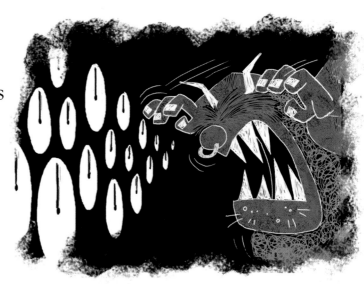

and put holes in socks!

But then Rabbit came up with a clever plan. They would collect things that the Backson liked and leave a trail of them to lure it into a pit. Then the Backson would be trapped—and they could get Christopher Robin back!

The rescue party set off, telling Owl they
hoped to be back soon. It occurred to Owl
that "back soon" sounded an awful lot
like **"Backson"**—a coincidence that
he found momentarily interesting,
though not terribly important.

While their friends went to gather the items that were needed, Pooh and Piglet picked up some supplies. Then the pair set off to choose the location for the all-important pit.

When they found the perfect spot, Pooh
and Piglet got straight to work. Piglet dug a
very deep pit. Next he covered it with a cloth,
then weighed down the corners of the
cloth with four large, heavy rocks.

"I almost forgot the most important part," said Piglet.

He took a honeypot and explained that they were going to

use it to help disguise the trap even more.

"Well, it certainly fooled me and my tummy," said Pooh.

The pair quickly caught up with the others, who were already leaving a trail of objects—socks, dishes, toys, and clocks, among many other things—across the Hundred-Acre Wood. Everyone worked together, knowing the sooner the trail was complete, the sooner the Backson would be captured—and the sooner Christopher Robin would be safe!

"Hurry along, everyone!" called Rabbit. "Don't dawdle."

Tigger, meanwhile, had decided to track the Backson on his own. He was pretty sure he had found him, too, when he pounced on something moving in the Wood. Unfortunately, it turned out to be Eeyore, who had accidentally been left behind by the others.

"You and me are gonna catch that Backson together!" Tigger declared.

"Do I have a choice?" asked Eeyore.

Tigger bounced off, thinking Eeyore was right behind him. But a few bounces later, Tigger discovered he was all alone.

Tigger returned to his friend. "Buddy," he said, "if you're gonna pounce, you gotta have some bounce. We just need to get you *tiggerized!*"

In his enthusiasm, Tigger didn't seem to realize that turning Eeyore into a tigger was sure to be a very large project indeed, because Eeyore was just about the most *un*-tiggerlike creature in the entire Hundred-Acre Wood.

Tigger started with the easy part: giving Eeyore stripes.

"Looking great," said Tigger. "Now you gotta learn to bounce like a tigger." He attached a large spring to Eeyore, and set him in motion.

The donkey went

up and down. . .

up and down. . .

up and down. . .

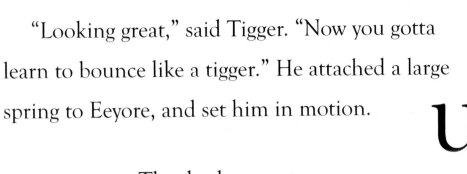

and, shortly thereafter, just up.

Back on the ground, Eeyore
continued to bounce out of control.

But Tigger was too caught up in the excitement
of his new project to take any notice!

Eventually, the friends ended up in Rabbit's garden. Tigger dressed up as the Backson and coached Eeyore on how a tigger would "bounce" the monster into surrendering. The poor donkey ricocheted from fence to scarecrow to clothesline to Tigger to the woods beyond.

Meanwhile, Pooh and Piglet and the other friends continued to lay their trail of items throughout the Wood.

RUMBLE! went Pooh's tummy, unhappy that honey had yet to come its way that day.

BUZZ! answered something overhead. It was a beehive! Pooh knew that, with Piglet's help, the honey inside could soon be his.

"Once I get you up in the tree, just hand me the beehive," Pooh instructed.

"I guess you've thought this through," said Piglet.

"Indeed I have," Pooh assured him as he jumped on the end of a log.

Piglet flew straight up—and became lodged deep inside the hive.

"Don't worry, Piglet," said Pooh. "I shall get you out."

"No hurry, Pooh," said Piglet good-naturedly. "The bees are quite gentle as long as there is no sudden movement."

WHAM! Pooh hit the beehive with a stick, hoping to dislodge it.

"Are you sure that's a good idea, Pooh?" asked Piglet.

"I'm quite sure," replied Pooh, whacking it again. WHAM!

"Well, you know best, Pooh," said Piglet.

Pooh didn't really—but at least it only took one more swipe of his stick to bring the hive down.

Angry bees quickly began to pour out.

"New plan, Piglet," announced Pooh. "Run!"

"Is this fast enough, Pooh?" Piglet asked.

The pair jumped off a small cliff and ran

into a very annoyed Rabbit.

"What are you two doing?" Rabbit demanded as he pulled the hive off Piglet. "Beehives are not on my list of Backson-friendly items." He tucked the beehive up into a tree and gave Pooh and Piglet a friendly shove. "Move along! Move along! We've so much to do!"

Over by Rabbit's house, Tigger searched for his new partner, Tigger II—also known as Eeyore.

Tigger didn't find Eeyore, but he did find Eeyore's spring "tail". "You're gonna need this if you're going to get the Backson. Unless the Backson got you first!"

Winnie the Pooh

Lost and Found

Rabbit was very pleased. His plan to catch the Backson and rescue Christopher Robin was almost complete! He and his friends had left a trail of items leading to the trap they had set for the Backson. Now all they had to do was wait for it to show up.

"Rabbit, can we stop for lunch?" Pooh asked.

"We cannot rest until Christopher Robin is found," insisted
Rabbit. "Try thinking of him instead of honey."

"Very well," Pooh agreed. He did his best to concentrate.

Then something very strange happened. Pooh's shadow
started looking like a honeypot!

Then, every time Pooh's friends spoke, all he could hear was, "Honey, honey, honey." Next, everything beneath Pooh's feet melted into a giant wave of honey! He swam and dived and floated in the honey. He gobbled and gulped and guzzled the honey. Pooh was so blissfully happy that he sang a honey song and danced a honey dance. Life was sweet!

POOF! Pooh's beautiful daydream faded. His honey ocean was really a muddy puddle—and Pooh was a great big mess! To make matters worse, it seemed his poor tummy would never get something to eat.

Pooh cleaned himself off and went on his way. After a few
steps, he came upon a large honeypot centered on a cloth. Pooh
was so excited at the prospect of honey that he didn't recognize
the very Backson trap he and Piglet had set earlier that day!

Pooh fell to the bottom of the pit, and before he could say "oh, bother," the honeypot fell on top of his head. Unfortunately for Pooh and his tummy, the pot was empty.

Meanwhile, Pooh's friends had arrived back
at the pit and were looking everywhere for him.
Then, all at once, they heard a loud *THUD!*
The friends clung to each other in fear.

"The plan worked!" Rabbit exclaimed. "We
caught the Backson!"

After each friend suggested that the other take a
look first, it was agreed that they would all go over to
the pit and look together.

"You went back for the honey, didn't you?" asked Piglet.
"I told you it was empty."

"Yes, and I believed you, Piglet," replied Pooh. "But my
tummy had to see for himself."

"How are we ever going to get him out?" wondered Kanga.

Just then, Eeyore arrived at the pit and showed off his
newest tail to the group.

Rabbit thought Eeyore's tail might be the answer to Pooh's predicament, so he threw the anchor into the pit.

It was so heavy, it yanked the friends down into the hole—and broke the honeypot on Pooh's head.

Only Piglet, who had been tossed high into the air, remained outside the trap.

"Oh, dear! Wait for me!" Piglet cried as he started to climb into the pit. He didn't want to be left alone with the Backson running around loose!

"No, Piglet!" Rabbit cried. "You can help us if you stay up there. Go look for something to get us out!"

Moments later, Piglet returned with a flower, but it was much too short to reach all the way down into the pit.

Next, Piglet brought a large book.

"You can't possibly think that's long enough," said Rabbit.

Piglet disagreed. "Owl read this to me once, and it was certainly the longest thing I'd ever heard."

On Piglet's third trip, he brought back a very useful rope. But, since there were six friends stuck in the pit, Piglet cut the rope into six equal pieces.

"Now you can all get out!" he said proudly.

But the pieces of rope were much too short to reach into the pit.

Just then, Roo remembered that Christopher Robin
owned a jump rope.

Rabbit urged Piglet to go to the boy's house and get it.

Owl flew out of the pit to encourage the terrified Piglet.
When he was done, he flew back in. It was now clear that
Owl did not need rescuing from the pit—but no one seemed
to notice.

Piglet, meanwhile, trudged nervously into the foggy woods, knowing he had a very important thing to do. As he looked all around, the very small animal backed into a very large tree root. Startled, he turned and saw what looked like a red-eyed monster glaring down from up in the tree. But it was only his friend B'loon.

Loyal little Piglet realized that no matter how frightened he was, he had to go back and save his friend.

Piglet slowly inched his way over to B'loon. A few tugs later, as Piglet pulled B'loon from the tree, an enormous shadow fell over them.

Piglet turned and faced the monster. "B-B-B-BACKSON!" he shouted. He held on tight to B'loon and raced away as fast as he could.

But there was no Backson—only Tigger dressed in a Backson disguise.

But now Tigger thought the Backson was right behind
him! He ran after his friend so that they could flee together.
"Piglet!" he cried.

"He knows my name!" shrieked Piglet. "HELP!"

B'loon lifted Piglet up and away, but it was a very bumpy
ride. Then Piglet spotted the pit in the distance. He thought
if he could just reach it—and his friends—he would be safe.
He had nearly made it when Tigger crashed into him.

Down into the pit they
both tumbled.

h
t
O
D
A
r
D
H
n
J
B
S
S
H
C
W

When the dust settled, everyone was relieved to see
that the "Backson" chasing Piglet was really only Tigger.
And Tigger was relieved to see all of his friends.

Suddenly, Tigger realized
he was sitting on Piglet!

"Sorry 'bout that, little
guy," Tigger said.

Just then, B'loon floated
up and out of Piglet's grasp.

"Don't leave!" called Rabbit.

"You're the only one who can
get us out of here!" Piglet explained.

Owl was not the least bit upset by the setback. He began to tell a very long story, unaware that his friends were growing bored. Pooh idly looked up and saw Tigger's discarded honeypot sitting at the edge of the pit. So he decided to build himself a ladder out of letters.

Back above ground, Pooh examined the honeypot. "Empty," he said as he tossed it over his shoulder.

Down

in

the

pit,

Owl was *still* talking! " . . . that the inkwell would launch into the air," he said. "And let me tell you, it packed quite a wallop!"

THUMP!
The honeypot
smacked the top
of Owl's head!

Suddenly, Rabbit saw Pooh's ladder of letters. "We can get out!" he cried.

The friends were relieved to be out of the pit—until they heard a rustling in the bushes.

"Backson!" they cried.

But it was only Christopher Robin, led by B'loon.

"How did you escape the Backson?" asked Rabbit.

"What on earth is a Backson?" Christopher Robin asked.

"The most wretched creature that you could meet," Owl said solemnly.

"What gave you the idea I was taken by a Backson?" replied Christopher Robin.

Pooh handed him the note. Christopher Robin giggled as he explained that he had written that he would be "back soon"—not "Backson." It had all been a misunderstanding!

Before the friends headed home, Rabbit declared, "We owe a very special someone a token of our appreciation. . . .

"Someone who got us out of this pit and helped us to find Christopher Robin. So, I bestow this pot of honey upon our dear friend . . . B'loon."

Pooh and his tummy were dumbstruck.

"Sorry, Pooh," said Eeyore.

"Ever have one of those days where you just can't win?"
Pooh asked.

Pooh's hungry tummy soon led him away, looking this
way and that for the honey it so desperately wanted.

Pooh kept on searching until he ended up at Owl's house.

It took all of Pooh's remaining energy to climb up the tree to Owl's front door, where he pulled the new bell rope. There was something very familiar about it.

As Owl invited Pooh in for some honey, he said, "I shall treat you to an excerpt from my memoirs, which tells the gripping tale of how only a few days ago I found that very handsome bell rope that you were admiring just hanging over a thistle bush. Nobody seemed to want it, so I brought it home."

"But somebody did want it, Owl," Pooh said. "My dear friend Eeyore. He was fond of it, you see. Attached to it."

"Of course. It is Eeyore's tail," said Owl realizing his mistake. "I was just keeping it safe for him."

As much as Pooh hated to leave the honey, he had to return Eeyore's tail to him right away.

Pooh took the tail straight to Christopher Robin, who securely attached it to Eeyore with a hammer and nail.

"What do you think?" Christopher Robin asked.

Eeyore considered his old tail, with which he was newly reunited. "Seems about the right length. Pink bow's a nice touch. Swishes real good, too," he said.

That was good enough for Christopher Robin. "Bring out the grand prize!" he instructed.

"Thank you all ever so much," said Pooh. He climbed straight into the pot. He swam and dived and floated in the honey. He gobbled and gulped and guzzled the honey. All his honey dreams had finally come true!

Later, Christopher Robin told Pooh how proud he was that Pooh had put his friend before his tummy.

"Thank you," Pooh replied. "I don't think I shall be hungry again for a good long while."

Just then, Pooh's stomach rumbled.

"Silly old bear!" said Christopher Robin.

The End